Sign up for a **FREE** Kauri the Kiwi coloring in page at

www.gemini-education.net

For my nephew Kauri.

Today is a beautiful sunny day
and Kauri the Kiwi wants to explore.
He better get ready
before he runs out the door.

Kauri tramps through the forest and past the trees.
He looks at the ferns and sees all their green leaves.

What sounds does Kauri make as he tramps?

Stomp
Crack
Stomp
Crack

Kauri comes to a huge white mountain
and starts hiking up.
Hopefully this mountain doesn't erupt.

What sound does Kauri make as he hikes in the snow?

Crunch
Crunch
Crunch
Crunch

Kauri gets to the top of the mountain and looks down.
He thinks it would be so much fun to slide around.

What sound does he make on the way down?

Swish

Swish

Swish

Swish

Kauri gets to a big blue lake
and swims to the other side.
He sees a wave
and catches a ride.

What sound does Kauri make as he swims?

Splash

Splash

Splash

Splash

Kauri walks past the boiling hot grey mud pools that smell like rotten eggs. He wishes he could block his nose from the smell with some pegs.

What does Kauri say as he walks past the mud pools?

Stinky

Stinky

Stinky

Stinky

Kauri walks past the
hot golden sand.
His feet are getting so hot
he wants to walk on his hands.

What does Kauri say as he walks on the sand?

Ouch

Ouch

Ouch

Ouch

Kauri finds a dark cave
and creeps around.
What is that in the darkness?
A scary sound!

Grrrrrrrr!

A big bad boar!

RUN!!!!!!

Over the hot golden sand!

Ouch

Ouch

Ouch

Ouch

Past the boiling hot grey mud pools!

Stinky

Stinky

Stinky

Stinky

Across the big blue lake!

Splash

Splash

Splash

Splash

Up the big white mountain!

Crunch

Crunch

Crunch

Crunch

Down the big white mountain!

Swish

Swish

Swish

Swish

Through the forest!

Stomp
Crack
Stomp
Crack

Safe back home.
What an exciting adventure!

The End.

Printed in Great Britain
by Amazon

85041628R00022